For the brave men and women of
law enforcement who have dedicated their
lives to the upholding of the law and the
protection of others.

In the Sheriff's office, each morning started with the Deputies receiving their assignments for the day.

"Deputy Knowles," said Sheriff Taylor, "Today you will be reading to children."

Deputy Knowles was delighted. Reading to children was one of her favorite things to do.

Shortly after that meeting, Deputy Knowles arrived at a local school. Everyone was thrilled to have someone from law enforcement as a guest.

The teachers greeted her and led her to the classroom in which she would be reading.

Deputy Knowles read the children one of their favorite books and used all kinds of funny voices that made them all laugh. Then, she asked if anyone had any questions.

A little girl named Alora raised her hand and asked, "Why do you wear a uniform?"

"That's a great question," Deputy Knowles replied.

"I wear a uniform like this
one to make it easy for others
to identify me as someone who
can help them with any issues
they may be having."

"What's that star on your chest?" asked a little boy named Justin.

"That star is a badge," answered Deputy Knowles. "All law enforcement officers wear a badge as a symbol of authority.

The five-point star is worn by most Deputy Sheriffs."

"What's that on your arm?" asked Abigail.

"This is a patch," said Deputy Knowles.

"All Virginia Deputies wear them. Each patch is different, depending on the department."

"Why do you have a gun?" asked Gabriel.

"I was wondering when someone was going to ask about that," Deputy Knowles responded with a smile.

"I carry a gun to protect you and me."

"But why do you carry two guns?" asked Liam.

"Actually, the second one is not a gun. It's an electronic device called a TASER, and it's very dangerous as well."

"Why do you always carry
a radio?" asked Owen.

"Our radios allow us to communicate with
other Deputies," answered Deputy Knowles.

"Do you ever arrest people?" asked Hayden.

"Sometimes," replied Deputy Knowles. "Everyone should obey the law, but some people don't and commit crimes that cause them to be arrested. Laws are like the rules you have to follow at school and at home."

"Does anyone have any other
questions?" asked Deputy Knowles.

A little girl named Bella raised her
Hand and said, "I like blueberries!"

Deputy Knowles smiled and responded, "I
like waffles." And all of the children laughed.

"I want to be a police officer when I grow up!" said Grayson.

"Not me," said Brayden. "I don't like police."

"Why don't you like police?" asked
Deputy Knowles.

"Because they're scary," said Brayden.

"Am I scary?" asked Deputy Knowles.

"No." answered Brayden. "But you do arrest people."

"You do know that Deputies do more than just arrest people, don't you?" asked Deputy Knowles.

"We are very involved in the community. Deputies provide food to homeless shelters, give away bike helmets to kids, find lost people...and, oh yeah...read to children!"

The End.

Made in the USA
Columbia, SC
08 May 2024

35360840R00020